SMITTEN BY THE ALIEN

GRACE KENSINGTON

1

—————

Dear Diary,

I still can't believe this is actually happening. One minute I was hiding at Zuri's house trying to decide what I was going to do next and being terrified that at any minute my evil son of a bitch of a stepfather was going to show up and kill me, and the next minute I was following Zuri and some warrior who is apparently in love with her to the university space shuttle to head to Uoria. I still can't believe how easily Ero made him go away.

I just re-read that sentence. I can't believe I am still not brave enough to even write his name. I am literally on another planet, nowhere near anywhere where he would be able to get near me, and I still can't bring myself to write it. Maybe one day I will get over everything that he has put me through since my idiot of a mother decided to marry him. I will never understand that.

What am I doing here? It seemed like a fantastic idea at the time when Zuri and Ero suggested that I come along with them when they returned to Uoria. Anything to get out of his line of fire for when he finally got over the shock of Ero scaring the living hell out of him. That and I really didn't have anywhere else to go and wasn't sure where I was going to live or what I was going to do for those little life details like food. Coming here was a way for me to stay with Zuri, who is the only person in the entire world that I trust, know that I will have somewhere to live and stay safe while I figure out what the hell I am going to do with my future, and use some of my chemistry and biology knowledge to actually do something good rather than just filling out tests.

I have only been on Uoria for a couple of hours and I am still so overwhelmed by everything that is going on. I thought that I would be spending time with Zuri, maybe getting a chance to talk to her about everything that had been going on with me in the last few weeks. As soon as we got here, though, Ero whisked her away somewhere and I got handed over to the human women and to a man named Ty. I was happy to see Leia, even though we don't know each other terribly well. To be honest, though, I was happier to see Ty. I wouldn't say this to anybody but you, but he is the most beautiful man I have ever seen in my entire life. He is huge beyond description and so gorgeous I couldn't even talk to him for the first few minutes. From what I understand, he is my own personal protector for while I'm here. That could make this experience much more pleasant.

I'm going to try to get some sleep. They gave me my own house to live in while I'm here, which is a major change from what I'm used to. There won't be anyone to bother me or to tell me what to do. Or to do anything else to me. Maybe I'll get lonely at some point, but for now this is all just too incredible for me to get my mind around. I might only have six months here before our exchange period ends and we have to go back to Earth, but I'm not going to think about that. I am going to take advantage of every moment that I have and deal with whatever is ahead of me when it comes.

Samira

I FINISHED my diary entry and tucked the notebook under my pillow. I know it is a completely outdated form of recordkeeping, but I had always found comfort in being able to actually write down my thoughts. I never read back through the stacks of notebooks I had accumulated throughout my eighteen years, but I figured that if I ever wanted to relive any of those moments, at least they would be there. On my darker days I figured that if my stepfather ever got his hands on me and I wasn't able to get away, at least the people who found me would have my journals to follow what had happened to me in the last several years of my life.

The house that the Denynso had put aside for me was small but comfortable and I settled back on the bed. It had taken some convincing for the human women to actually leave me alone in the house rather than staying with me and helping me get settled in. I didn't want to be rude to them, but the last thing I wanted that night was to sit around and regale them with the stories of what led up to coming with Zuri. For now, I was more than happy to let them believe that I was just another exchange student who had joined the program for people of Earth to come to Uoria and exchange knowledge, ideas, and cultural traditions. Unless I had the chance to spend time with Zuri, I would rather be alone. Well, Zuri or Ty.

As soon as I saw Ty, I knew that I wanted to spend

more time with him. He didn't have the gruff, aggressive feeling that the other men did and I found myself wondering if he was a warrior like Pyra and Gyyx, the Denynso mates of Eden and Leia, or if he was something else like Ciyrs, the mate of Eliana. The three human women seemed so happy with their Denynso men, and I found myself curious about the quiet, calm man entrusted with guiding me to my house and who said he would be my guide and protector while I was on Uoria. I wanted to know more about him, to find out what lurked behind those eyes and gave him an energy and presence that made me feel almost safe and comfortable near him.

2

"What the hell is wrong with me?" Ty asked, pouring a few more ingredients into the huge bowl in front of him and going at it with a spoon with such intensity Pyra took a step back.

"What do you mean?" the enormous warrior asked.

Ty paused his assault of the cake batter and looked at Pyra.

"If you haven't noticed, my apron has a bit of a tent situation going on here and I haven't been able to think straight since last night."

Pyra glanced down at the front of Ty's apron and saw exactly what he was talking about. Though better concealed with the thick white apron hanging over him than it would have been if he was just standing there in the soft tie-front pants that were the usual wardrobe of the Denynso men, it was still pretty obvious that he had a raging hard-on. The baker shifted slightly and Pyra looked up at him with a knowing grin.

"Yeah, I've noticed. Why are you even asking? You

watched me go through it months ago, then Ciyrs, then Gyyx, and now Ero. It seems that the efforts to communicate and cooperate more effectively with Earth have had a much different impact than we originally anticipated. These human women get here and the Denynso men start dropping like flies. It looks like you are the one that came under the line of fire this time."

He reached out and dipped a finger in the bowl of batter and Ty pulled it away from him roughly. Even though he was baking a cake specifically for Pyra to bring to his mate Eden, who happened to be a couple of months into her first pregnancy and constantly in the throes of either a dramatic emotional situation or a craving, Ty didn't like when Pyra stuck his fingers in the batter. Not only did it just seem pretty unsanitary, his perfectionist ways made Ty feel like it threw off the entire balance and measurement of the batter so the cake wouldn't turn out exactly as he had wanted it to when he first started baking it. In the back of his mind he knew that that was being a little bit ridiculous, but he couldn't help it. Just like the warriors couldn't shake off their compulsion to fight and protect, Ty couldn't fight off his compulsion to create and perfect.

"That can't possibly be it," Ty said, adding a few drops of dark brown liquid from a bottle he kept on the top shelf of his spice cabinet.

"Why not? I was there when Zuri got back with that new girl. Anyone with eyes can see that she's beautiful."

"Samira."

"What?" Pyra asked, running the tip of one of his fingers through a mound of sweet powder on the counter and licking it off.

"The new girl. Her name is Samira."

"Uh-huh. I guess your big old orange eyes definitely noticed that she's beautiful."

"My eyes aren't orange!" Ty protested, then picked up a cookie sheet so he could see his reflection. Sure enough, there were streaks of orange through the usual brown of his eyes. "Shit."

"Yep. They might not have made their complete changeover yet, but those eyes cannot deceive. They know that your mate has shown up, and unless you are preparing yourself to fight Ero for Zuri or you are going to break into the space shuttle and try to pry out that little flight attendant who always runs and hides the minute that the ship lands, that means that your mate is Samira."

"She can't be."

"I don't get it. Why are you so pissed about your mate showing up? You have the whole nurturing and taking care of someone thing down pat. You've been taking care of all of us warriors for as long as I can remember. And you are plenty old enough to get mated."

Ty groaned and started distributing the batter into three hexagonal pans he had placed in a row in the middle of the counter.

"That's the problem right there. I am plenty old enough, but is she? Did you see her? She looks barely old enough to be out of her mother's house much less in somebody's bed. I just don't feel right looking at her the way that I obviously look at her when she is so young."

"She's old enough to be Zuri's student, which means that she is old enough to be in college. I don't think that Zuri would have brought her here if she wasn't an adult, but if it makes you feel any better, I can ask Eden how old she is exactly."

"How would she know that?"

"They are human women. They tell each other everything. It's a little disturbing actually. I think that she had told the other girls far more than I would ever want any of them to know about me because last time I was in the room with all of them, they all seemed to be far too focused on the front of my pants. And since I am no longer in the fun pre-mating phase that you are currently finding yourself enjoying, there would be nothing to draw their attention there unless they were trying to confirm a story that they heard."

Ty laughed, feeling better now that he at least had Pyra to commiserate with him a little bit. It wasn't exactly the same thing, but they had both found themselves at the mercy of the confounding and sometimes irresistible human women who had started infiltrating their planet.

As he slipped the cakes into the oven, Ty found his mind wandering back to Samira. The second she stepped off the shuttle from the university the night before, he was enraptured. This was something he had never felt before. While some of the warriors were known for having as many female conquests as they did battle victories, Ty had never been that kind of man. He had thought he had feelings for a couple of the females of the tribe a few times before, but even when they had sex no bonding ever occurred. Now that he had seen Samira, he realized that those feelings were nothing and that he was truly screwed. If Pyra was right, and truth be told, Pyra was almost always right, especially when it came to things that he had experienced himself, there was nothing that

Ty could do about his newfound attraction to Samira. If the constant erection wasn't enough to tell him, the hint of orange in his eyes was unmistakable.

Samira was his mate and would be the only one for him for the rest of his life. He would just have to decide if he could deal with it or if he was going to let her age keep him from pursuing her and risk living the rest of his existence alone and longing for her. It was not a decision that he wanted to make.

3

When I woke up the morning after arriving on Uoria, I had a few disorienting moments when I had no idea where I was. In the first few seconds after I woke up but before I opened my eyes I thought that I might still be at Zuri's house, and then I had a moment of panic thinking that I was back at my mother's house and that the pounding I heard was my stepfather knocking on the door trying to get into my bedroom. My eyes snapped open and I saw the unfamiliar room around me and I was briefly terrified. Finally, I regained my senses and remembered that I was in Uoria in my own little house, and that I was, for once, safe.

After just a few seconds of feeling calm and in control again, however, I heard the loud pounding and again became afraid. I sat up in the bed and pulled the covers up around me, pulling my knees to my chest like I always did when I felt scared. It was a protective position that made me feel like I was retracting into my shell. Too many memories of nights spent just like that in my bed at home, or in the corner of my bedroom, or even, on particularly horrible nights, curled in the closet just like that so that I could try to guard myself as much as I could.

"Samira?"

I heard my name added to the pounding and instantly recognized the voice as belonging to Ty. He was standing at the front door to my house, knocking insistently on the door and calling me. When I listened to his voice, however, I realized that it was not anger or frustration, but genuine concern and worry for me that was causing him to call out to me so loudly. I gathered my blankets close around me and hurried across the house to the door.

"Yes?" I said, pulling the door open and stepping behind it as much as I could to conceal myself while still being able to look at him.

I could see Ty's eyes scanning what of my body he could see and then snap up to mine, a look that somehow combined intrigue and shame crossing his face. He was even more gorgeous now that I was looking at him in daylight. Rather than the Mohawk style I had seen among most of the other men, Ty wore his stark white hair down and loose except for a braid down the center of his head that reached to the base of his neck. I am not a small woman, yet he towered over me, making me feel small and delicate. This was something I had never felt, and I loved it. I wanted to explore more of it, to see just how powerful he was and how well he knew how to use that power.

"Ty?" I said, realizing that he hadn't said anything since I opened the door.

He shook his head hard like he was trying to bring his

thoughts back into reality and gestured behind him.

"The king and queen want you to come to meet them and to have breakfast in the meeting hall. Usually human visitors have to report to them first, but since you were a bit of a surprise, they weren't in the hall last night when you arrived and said that it was fine to have your greeting this morning."

I was confused by the formality of it, and by being described as a "surprise".

"I thought that Zuri told everyone that I was coming."

"She did, but we didn't get the communication until right before your arrival. Ero sent the message when he arranged transport back here, but the transportation officials didn't let us know until the day before you got here. "

"I don't understand. If they didn't tell everybody that I was coming, how did they have a house ready for me and how did they choose you as my guard?"

A bit of panic was starting to build in my chest. It was that feeling of being out of place and unwanted. I didn't want to be an imposition to anyone and my mind was suddenly reeling with plans for how I was going to get myself back to Earth now that the shuttle was already preparing to leave and there was no way I would be able to get back on it before take-off.

"You aren't an imposition," Ty said and then suddenly looked shocked.

I looked at him, stunned. He had just responded to what I was thinking, using my exact words to comfort me.

"How did you know that I was thinking that?"

He stuttered for a few seconds like he was trying to

come up with words to explain what had just happened, and then I noticed his eyes had dropped again. Without realizing it, I had stepped out from behind the door and was standing fully in front of him. My blankets had slipped down slightly and he could plainly see that I sleep naked with the top of the blanket barely covering my nipples and the two sides wrapped around me closed just beneath the apex of my thighs. His eyes lifted to mine and felt my breath deepen slightly. I had known this man for just a few hours, but in that moment, all I wanted was for him to touch me. The feeling was overwhelming, deep and intense like it was something that had always been in me but that I was just discovering.

Instead of fulfilling that wish, however, Ty turned his eyes away from me and cleared his throat softly. I gathered my blankets closer around me reluctantly and stepped backwards into the house.

"Do you want to come in while I get dressed?"

He shook his head.

"I'll just wait here."

Feeling slightly hurt, I closed the door and went back to my bedroom to get dressed. I wasn't sure what to wear. He had mentioned the king and queen, but I knew from Zuri that they weren't like the kings and queens you hear about from history classes at Earth. She described them as kind and approachable, people who associated with the rest of the tribe that they ruled with compassion, affection, and respect. Still, they were the monarchs and I didn't want to offend them with my clothing. I wished Zuri were there to help me.

Suddenly I felt like I heard Ty's voice in my head

telling me that I would look beautiful in anything. It sent a shiver down my spine and brought a flutter to my belly. Smiling to myself for reasons that I didn't fully understand at the time, I draped my blankets back over my bed and dressed.

4

Dammit, dammit, dammit, dammit, dammit.

Ty sighed and sagged back against the door to Samira's house. How could he be so stupid? Tuning into the thoughts of another person was extremely intimate, which is why it was something that only mates, with a few very specific exceptions, shared. It was part of the bond that occurred between the men of his kind and their women, and it allowed them to stay fully connected. This could be very helpful when they needed to find each other, when one needed the help of the other, or they wanted to express something private to each other without anyone else hearing it.

The fact that he could already connect with Samira was startling to say the least, considering they had never even touched each other much less bonded. Now he had been dumb enough to not only listen to her thoughts, but reply to her both speaking to her and sending his own thoughts to her. He knew he was probably scaring the hell out of her, or at the very least making her think that she was crazy. He hadn't even decided yet what he was going to do about these intense feelings he was experiencing for the stunning but so young woman that was now dressing in the house behind him. This was not a good time to start toying with her by listening to her thoughts and sending her his without her understanding what was going on.

He had been chastising himself for a few minutes when he felt the door give way behind him and fell back. Samira let out a scream and he turned as he fell so that he came down on his hands rather than on his back. His fall had caused her to fall and land on her back, which meant that he landed over her, his hands on either side of her and his face level with hers. They lay there for a few tense seconds, staring at each other. Their breaths came out ragged, mingling between them and surrounding them with a sound that only partially concealed the pounding of their heartbeats.

Ty could see something flicker in her eyes. It looked like desire and when she licked her lips, he almost lost the control he had been struggling so hard to maintain around her. She was even more startlingly beautiful when he was this close to her, but she still looked so young. He felt like he would be taking advantage of her if he gave into his craving for her at that moment, and if he did that he would never be able to forgive himself.

She was not tiny like Eden, Eliana, or Leia, but taller like Zuri. The extra inches made it so that their bodies lined up perfectly and he had to move extremely carefully to get out of the position hovering over her so that she didn't feel his raging cock pressing down on her. It was like it had a mind of its own, straining against his pants as it tried to get to her, just knowing that hers was the body it was made for.

"I'm sorry," he muttered, climbing backwards and standing up.

He wanted to reach down to help her up, but he worried about being able to maintain his self-control if he touched her in that moment. It was already taking everything that he had not to sweep her off her feet and carry her back into the bedroom where he could spend the rest of the day bonding with her. He didn't want to test his capacity to withhold himself if he touched her skin, even just her hand, in that second.

"It's alright," she said, standing up and brushing herself off, "I'm sorry I didn't realize you were leaning against the door."

He looked at her fully and saw that she had put on a pair of tight black pants and a black shirt that hugged her curves and dipped low over her breasts, creating an enticing swell of cleavage. His mouth watered and he felt his heart start to pound. They needed to get out of her house as soon as possible.

A FEW MINUTES later they were walking through the compound toward the meeting hall. Ty noticed that she was able to keep up with him without struggle thanks to her long legs and a fast pace that made her breasts bounce and her long, thick hair sway across her back. Suddenly she turned to him.

"You never answered me when I asked how the house was ready for me if nobody knew I was coming until right before I got here."

"That house was originally intended for Zuri. It was the one chosen for her when she came here the first time for her teaching position, and when she left so suddenly it was just left there without anybody living in it. We assumed that whoever took her place as the new exchange program professor would end up moving into that house, but then we found out that Ero had gone after her and that she would be returning with him."

"So, if that is the house that was supposed to be hers, where is she living now that she's back?"

Ty glanced at her strangely. He assumed the human girls would have filled her in on all of the gossip from the planet, especially the mating between Zuri and Ero considering she was Zuri's friend.

"She's with Ero. She's his mate, that's why he went after her."

"His mate?" she asked, sounding surprised.

"They didn't tell you any of this?"

"Everything was kind of a whirlwind. I wasn't even expecting to see Zuri again for months. I had no idea that she had come home so quickly after leaving. I was staying in her house after an issue with my stepfather and she showed back up, and then the next morning Ero got there and it was all very fast after that. I didn't ask any questions."

He could see the hurt and fear in her eyes and felt the need to comfort her. Ty lifted an arm and rested it gently around her shoulders. He worried that she would pull away from him or be intimidated, but she didn't. Instead, she seemed to relax a bit at his touch. She stepped a little bit closer to him so that her hip brushed his as they walked.

"May I ask what happened with your stepfather?"

He wasn't even sure what the term meant, but from the way she said it he could tell that whoever that man was, he had done something terrible to her. Samira must have noticed the hint of uncertainty in his voice because she glanced up at him with a smile.

"You don't know what a stepfather is, do you?"

Part of him wanted to pretend that he did so that he didn't look dumb in front of her, but at the same time, he knew that the goal of the exchange program with Earth was to bring humans over so that they could educate the Denynso about the cultures, customs, and history of the planet and its people so she was probably not surprised that he was unsure of some of what she said. Finally, he shook his head.

"My mother and my father got divorced when I was pretty young, then she married...," she hesitated as if she couldn't bring herself to say the word that was right at the tip of her tongue. She closed her eyes and let out a breath, "she married her second husband, which is what a stepfather is. Does that make sense?"

She didn't say it like she was mocking him and Ty realized that he really enjoyed learning more about the other planet, even if it was something that broke his heart even to think about.

"I guess. I mean, I get what you are saying, but I have to admit I don't really understand it. We don't have divorce among the Denynso."

She looked surprised.

"You don't? Everybody just stays married no matter what?"

"Well, no. We don't get married. We bond. There is

only one other person in the entire existence that can create a bond with each of us, and once we have found that mate and complete the bond, it is for life. There is no such thing as two mated people just deciding that they no longer want to be mates and then finding new mates. They are with their mates, or they are alone. That's just the way it is."

She got a soft, almost sad look in her eyes and Ty stopped walking so that he could turn her to face him. He wanted to be closer to her, just to look at her. The feelings building inside him were threatening to overwhelm him, and even though he felt guilty for even thinking about her that way, he needed to feel her near him.

"And they're happy?" she asked, looking up at him.

Ty nodded, reaching up to brush a strand of her dark hair away from her face. He traced the curve of her jawline with one fingertip. She was so beautiful. He had never seen any woman that looked like her, that was so breathtaking he literally couldn't stop looking at her.

"I have never seen Pyra, Gyyx, Ciyrs, or Ero as happy as they are now. Finding our mate is something that we look forward to our entire lives. We know that once we find her, we will be complete. The bond is something that can't be broken and I have never known a mated pair to ever be unhappy together."

"Never?"

"I mean, they argue, of course. There's always going to be bickering and disagreements between people who truly love each other. They don't last, though. Nothing keeps them from wanting to be together."

As they spoke their bodies had drawn closer to each other and Ty could see her trembling slightly. He touched her face again, bringing his fingers beneath her chin so he could tilt her face up to look at him again. He wondered if she could feel it too; if she understood what was happening between them and what it meant. She tilted her face so that her cheek pressed further into his palm and Ty started to ask her what she was feeling when he heard someone shouting his name from behind them.

5

———————

The sound of the deep, gruff voice calling Ty's name jolted me out of the peaceful calm that he had created between us and I stepped back away from him. His hand fell away from my face and I immediately missed his touch. He was so incredibly sweet, so caring and attentive in a way that I had never experienced. When he talked about the mated couples and how happy they were together, I felt my heart reaching out to him, seeming to melt with each of his words. There was something in the way he was saying them that made it feel like he was telling me much more than just about how they created partnerships in his culture.

What really stood out to me about what he had said was the concept of bonding as opposed to marriage. He hadn't explained what the bonding was or how they went about knowing that they both wanted to bond, and I was desperate to find out. The way he talked about it was so reverent and mysterious, but at the same time, when he said it I could feel a primal heat and energy come off of him. My body responded instantly and again I felt the need for him to touch me. It was unlike anything I had ever felt about another guy. The teenage boys that flocked around me and even the older students at the university had been a bore and even though I dated, I never felt a strong connection to anyone. Now all I could think about was Ty and the way I craved him.

"Tyant!"

The booming voice sounded intense and demanding, almost like whoever was yelling was trying to be forceful and intimidating to whoever was around to listen, but particularly to Ty. I saw Ty's eyes close briefly before he turned around to face the man walking toward us. He had the Mohawk of the other men and the long stride of a warrior. I immediately tensed. Pyra, Gyyx, and Ero seemed nice in the very brief time that I had had to interact with them, but I was quickly finding that I didn't like the other warriors very much. Their aggressive, almost violent personalities made me feel the same type of crushing oppression that I had become accustomed to feeling from my stepfather and I was not about to let myself feel that again when I had just so narrowly escaped him. I came here to get away from the things that frightened me and held me back, if only for a little while, and the thought of them putting me right back into that feeling was something I couldn't tolerate.

"The king and queen want you now," the man said as he approached.

He wasn't looking at Ty, but at me. I saw his eyes scour over my body and lock on my mouth. He licked his lips and I felt my body stiffen uncomfortably. There was none of the gentleness, the connection in his eyes that was in Ty's, and I noticed that his eyes remained a dark purple color rather than shifting occasionally to orange as I noticed that Ty's did.

Ty stepped up closer to me and I felt myself leaning toward him.

"We're on our way," Ty said.

"Maybe I should take over from here," the man said, "After all, shouldn't our lovely new guest have a warrior to protect her like the other human women have?"

"Ciyrs isn't a warrior," Ty said.

"Ciyrs didn't escort Eliana when she first came here. Pyra did. But as we know, Pyra is extremely mated and has a little more on his plate than the rest of us do, so there seems to be a position open that requires a warrior to step in and take over. You did a fine job getting her to her house, but I'll take it from here. Why don't you go on back home and bake something?"

The words were so vicious that even I felt the venom coming off of them and I shifted uncomfortably. I didn't feel like a person in that moment, but more like a toy that these two men were batting around between them, trying to gain dominance over the other.

"She was given to me," Ty protested.

"Excuse me?" I said, taken aback by the words coming out of Ty, "Given to you? Is that what you men do on this planet? Just gather up the women as they step off the shuttles from Earth and hand them out like party favors?"

Tears were stinging in my eyes and I felt like I couldn't be near either of the men anymore. While I was furious with the warrior for his arrogance, I was heartbroken by Ty. He had been so sweet and suddenly he seemed just like all of the other men who had come my way.

I took off running, not entirely sure where I was going but confident that I would be able to find my way to the meeting hall on my own. Going on my understanding of patterns and grids, I used my instincts to weave my way through the compound until it opened out into a large space with a towering building at its center. I saw Zuri standing on the steps leading up to the front door with Ero standing a few steps beneath her, his head rested on her stomach as he held her around her hips.

I ran toward her, part of me feeling horrible for breaking up the beautiful moment between the couple. She looked up and noticed me. Gently easing Ero away from her, she came to meet me, gathering me in her arms even before she spoke.

"What's wrong?" she asked.

I shook my head and tried to explain what had just happened. I could feel the eyes of the other men on me and I found myself longing for Ty even though I was still upset with him. At least with him nearby I felt like I was protected.

"Where is he?" the enormous warrior I remembered from the night before as Pyra stalked toward me.

"I left him near my house," I answered.

"And you said he was with a warrior?" I nodded, "And he insulted you?"

"Not me, really. More Ty, I guess. He told him that he would take over from there and that he should be the one that was guarding me."

"Oh, shit."

Without any more warning than that, Pyra shot off in

the direction of my house, Ero following even faster after him.

"What was that all about?" I asked Zuri.

She stroked my hair and smiled at me. I could see something different about her, but I wasn't sure what.

"Can I ask you a question, Samira?"

"Of course."

"What color are Ty's eyes when he looks at you?"

"Sometimes they're brown and sometimes they're orange."

Her smile grew slightly and she nodded, looping her arm through mine and guiding me toward the door to the meeting hall.

"Let's get you inside to meet with the king and queen and then get some breakfast. I think we have a few things to talk about."

6

"Look what you did," Dillyn said tauntingly, "You made the pretty little thing run away. Well, maybe not so little. Young, though. Fresh and tender just like..."

Before he could get another word out, Ty's fist connected with his cheek and Dillyn went sprawling across the ground. The impact sent a surge of adrenaline through Ty and he launched at the prone warrior, tackling him down into the dirt before Dillyn could even get his wits about him again. He could barely believe what he was doing, but Ty couldn't stop his attack. The anger and protectiveness that filled him was unlike anything he had ever felt. Usually calm and docile, he had always been a nurturer, not a fighter. Suddenly, though, he had discovered the beast inside him. As soon as Dillyn started talking about Samira that way, he had felt like something inside him had unfurled like a tightly wound metal spring that someone suddenly released.

He continued to wail on Dillyn, pounding him into

the ground with all of the fury that boiled within him. After a few moments, he felt a tug on his shoulder and his name coming through the loud ringing in his ears.

"Damn, Ty, get off of him!"

He felt another hand on his other shoulder and the combination of the two finally pulled him away from Dillyn. The warrior writhed on the ground, blood pouring from his face and streaked across his chest. It felt like his constantly present erection had gotten even harder and now Ty was so filled with energy and adrenaline all he wanted to do was find Samira, toss her over his shoulder, and bring her back to his house. In the back of his mind, though, he could still hear Dillyn talking about how young she was. The conflict made him feel sick and he needed to get away from the situation.

He pushed past Pyra and Ero, heading for his shop. It was the one place where he felt completely comfortable and could get out his stress in a way other than beating the shit out of a warrior for upsetting Samira and then talking about her in such a disrespectful way. He heard the two warriors fall into step behind him, but that was fine. He didn't mind them coming along. In fact, he thought it might be nice to have them to talk to. Since they were both recently mated they might be able to help him navigate all of his confusion. He thought that maybe they would be able to talk him out of his compulsive need for Samira.

"She's 18, Ty," Pyra said as soon as they stepped into the shop behind Ty.

"Holy shit," Ty said, resting his elbows on the counter and burying his head in his hands, "She's only 18."

"That's an adult," Pyra reminded me, "and she is far

smarter than other women her age. You really are not that much older than she is. I don't understand why this is stressing you out so much."

Ty raised his head and looked at the two warriors standing in front of them. These were men he had been taking care of for years, using his unusual talents and strengths to nurture them and make sure that they had what they needed. He was like Ciyrs in a way, but whereas Ciyrs healed them if they were sick or injured, Ty took care of them while they were well and helped to make sure they stayed that way. It was not what people expected of a Denynso of his size, but it suited him. Now he was feeling more like one of the aggressive, violent warriors and it was all because he was struggling between knowing he had found his mate and not knowing if it was right to pursue her.

"What if I hurt her? What if she isn't ready to handle all of this and she ends up going back to Earth?"

"I just went through that exact situation," Ero reminded him.

"I know, but you went after her and she came back. Zuri is a grown woman. She knows who she is and what she wants out of life. She made the decision to leave you, but she also made the decision to come back to you. What if Samira leaves and is too afraid to come back? I don't think I could stand knowing that I had hurt her or taken advantage of her in some way while trying to bond with her, and then having to be alone for the rest of my life."

"Here's the thing, Ty," Ero said, "I didn't know if Zuri was actually going to come back with me, but I had to try. You already know that Samira is your mate. Whether you bond with her now or 5 years from now when she's your age, she will still be your mate and she will still be linked to you forever. Remember, though, that 5 years from now, she will be older, but so will you. When is it going to be right? And are you willing to possibly lose her forever because you were too afraid?"

Ty didn't have a chance to respond before he saw a figure appear in the doorway.

"We're going to head out of here," Pyra said, taking Ero by the arm and dragging him out of the room.

"Hi, Samira," Ero said as he struggled to keep up with Pyra.

"Hi, Ero," she replied, and then turned to Ty, "Hi, Ty."

"Hi," he said, turning the bread dough he had been working on out onto the counter.

"What are you doing?" she asked, taking a few steps toward him.

"Making bread," he answered shortly, still not looking up at her.

Suddenly he felt her come up beside him and rest a hand on his upper arm.

"Can I help?" she asked softly.

7

I watched Ty's hands kneading into the dough on the counter and felt the flutter in my belly grow more intense. His powerful hands worked over the dough masterfully, and I wanted them on my body. The conversation I'd had with Zuri resonated through my mind, and as I looked at him, I knew my dear friend and professor was right. This big, beautiful man was my mate, and after Zuri had given me a careful explanation of exactly what it entailed, I knew that I wanted more than anything to bond with him.

I touched his arm, feeling the muscles tense and shift beneath his skin as he continued to press into the dough. His rhythm seemed to increase a little and I lifted his arm so that I could slip beneath it. He cleared his throat, but lowered his arms around me so that his hands rested over mine. Lifting them up, he brought them down onto the dough and guided me in kneading it. The dough felt soft and warm beneath my hands, and Ty's hands felt strong and comforting over them. I could feel the heat from his body radiating toward mine, and with each long press down into the dough, his erection brushed against me.

The feeling of it made me moan softly and I arched my back to press my hips back toward him so that I returned the touch with more intensity and intention. His hands pushed mine deeper into the dough, kneading harder as his breath dropped and I could hear him struggling to control it behind me. I leaned back so that my back touched his chest, subtly rolling my hips against him. His breath caught in his throat and his hands stopped moving.

"Samira," he said imploringly.

"Yes, Ty?"

"Stop."

"Why?"

I rolled my hips a little harder and heard him groan.

"This isn't right."

"Why?"

I was going to force him to tell me exactly what he was thinking so that I could prove how wrong he was. I knew exactly why he thought it was wrong. Zuri had learned from Pyra that he was upset about my age. I didn't care what he thought, though. I had fallen for Ty as soon as I saw him and there was no way that I was going to let a few years of difference between us keep from having him as my mate. I would just have to prove how much of a woman I really was.

"You're too young," he finally whispered.

I pressed back into him and tilted my head so I could kiss his neck.

"Am I? Do I feel too young to you?"

Ty gave a soft grunt and I withdrew my hands from the dough, brushing the flour off of them.

"No," he said gruffly.

I turned around to face him. The orange streaks in his eyes were covering more of the brown now and I felt a surge in my heart as I remembered that Zuri told me the Denynso men's eyes changed to orange when they mated. I knew I was getting to him. I just had to press further. I touched his face gently, easing it forward with my fingertips against his cheek until I could touch my mouth to his. My lips parted and I touched the tip of my tongue to his bottom lip, tempting him to open his mouth. When he did, I flicked my tongue across his, deepening the kiss briefly before pulling back, catching his bottom lip between my teeth as I went.

"Do I kiss like I'm too young?" I asked, my voice dropping the more I spoke.

He shook his head and I smiled, leaning in to kiss him again. He returned the kiss, but only slightly as if still struggling to control himself.

"Please, Samira," he said, his eyes closed.

"Look at me, Ty," I said and he opened his eyes, "Do I look like I'm too young?"

His eyes grew sad and he nodded.

"Yes."

"Do I?" I asked, taking the hem of my shirt and pulling it off over my head.

"We're in my shop, Samira," he said, "Anybody could walk in at any second and see you."

"I want you to see me."

"I can see you."

His defenses were dropping and I was eager to keep going.

"Your house is connected to the shop, isn't it?" I asked, referencing what Zuri had told me.

"Yes."

I walked across the shop to the door on the back wall. I knew it led directly into his house and that he rarely locked it. That afternoon was the same as usual and the door opened easily beneath my hand. I glanced over my shoulder at him as I stepped into his house.

"Where is your bedroom, Ty?"

He didn't answer and I stepped all the way into the house, deciding I would just figure out where the room was on my own. After a few seconds, he hadn't followed me. I unbuttoned and unzipped my pants and pulled them off, tossing them back through the door into the shop. They hit the ground and I heard Ty groan. The door swung open further and I saw his broad form fill the doorway. I had undressed myself down to nothing but a black lace bra and matching panties, and when he looked at me, his eyes went completely orange.

"Do I look too young now?"

He still didn't answer and I turned away from him, giving him a full view of all of my curves in the barely-there panties, and walked further into the house. I glanced around and saw a stairwell in the far corner. I crossed to it and climbed the stairs slowly, letting my hips sway with each step. I could feel him following me, his eyes on my body as I put myself on display for him. I wanted him to want me with the same fire and intensity that I wanted him, and when I was finished with him, I wanted him to have no question left in his mind whether I was old enough to be his mate.

I made it up the stairs and found that almost the entire upper floor was his bedroom. A massive bed sat in the middle of a huge room, making it look like a pedestal where I was more than ready to worship. I turned to face him as Ty stepped into the room.

"Come closer," I told him.

He seemed reluctant, but he complied, closing the space between us with a few long, slow steps. I kissed him, drawing his tongue into my mouth and sucking on it suggestively as I pressed the front of my body to his. I could feel his erection pushing into my belly and I nudged against him.

"Undress me," I said.

I felt his hands shaking slightly as he brought them to my back to release the hooks on my bra. He peeled it away from my body and dropped it to the floor at our feet, and then hooked his fingers in the waistband of my panties to ease them off of my hips. I wriggled them off of my legs and stepped out of them, now completely bare in front of him.

Walking backwards, I made my way to the bed. When I felt the edge of the mattress on the backs of my legs, I turned around and crawled onto the bed, arching my back as I went. I reached the pillows and turned so I reclined back on them.

"Take off your shirt."

He complied and I felt my body clench at the sight of his chiseled chest and rippled stomach. I wanted to get my hands on him so badly, but I was determined that it was going to be him that took me. I might be seducing him, but when we finally did bond, he was going to be the one that made it happen.

"Everything else," I said, fighting to keep my voice steady.

His eyes glowed back at me and I could see the struggle continuing behind them as he at once fought his desire for me and gave in to my seduction. My mouth watered when I finally saw his fully naked body, his muscles beautifully formed under smooth skin, and his perfect, powerful-looking erection standing out from his hips in a way that made me almost lose control. I licked my lips and I saw Ty's cock twitch.

"Oh," I said, "Is that what you want?"

I beckoned him forward with one finger, encouraging him to climb onto the bed with me. He laid down beside me and I got on my knees between his legs, reaching forward to finally wrap my hand around his gorgeous erection. My fingers couldn't touch as I encircled his thick shaft and the tingle between my thighs spiked. I leaned down and drew my tongue along the underside of him from the base to the tip, then licked again to gather the drop of crystalline fluid that had gathered there. He groaned and I met the sound with the slide of my mouth over the head.

I slipped down further, moving slowly to savor every vein and ridge against my lips and tongue. Holding the base in one hand, I picked up a smooth, steady rhythm that brought him further and further into my mouth with each glide. My attention wrenched groans from his chest and soon Ty was gripping the comforter on either side of him, his eyes squeezed closed as he concentrated on the sensations I was sending through him. I could feel him getting harder in my mouth and I released him, giving him a few seconds to cool to bring him back from the brink.

Moving forward, I straddled his hips, settling myself so my pelvis touched his and my core cradled his erection. I rested his cock against my palm and rocked my hips, causing me to slide up and down him. The hot wetness from my body transferred to his, making my movements silky and easy. With each rock, I brought my core further up his shaft, eventually getting to a point where the tip teased my clit with each stroke. The breath caught in my throat at that feeling and I repeated it, pressing up slightly with my palm to increase the pressure between our bodies.

"Do I feel too young?" I asked. He didn't answer and I pressed harder, burrowing him in my folds without letting him enter me, "Do I, Ty?"

Suddenly he grabbed me by my hips and flipped me onto my back. I gasped at the movement and felt my body get even wetter as he hovered over me, staring down into my face with intensity that took my breath away.

"No," he growled and I felt the tip of his erection tease at my opening.

"Are you my mate, Ty?" I whispered.

He moved his hips forward slightly, massaging me and building pressure low in my belly.

"I am your mate."

"Do you want me?"

"More than anything I have ever wanted in my life."

I took a long, shuddering breath.

"Show me."

He pushed forward and filed me, taking his time to let

me stretch around him. I whimpered at the intense feeling and clutched at his back. Just when I thought I couldn't accommodate any more, Ty gave a hard thrust, sinking all the way into me and eliciting a sharp cry at the blissful combination of pain and pleasure. We paused there for a moment, letting our bodies learn each other. He kissed me languidly, his mouth moving across my familiarly.

Finally, his hips relaxed and I felt him start to move within me. My walls held him firmly and he groaned deeply as he built his rhythm. Each long, deep thrust coaxed sounds from my lips and I gave myself over to him, allowing him to bond me to him completely and irrevocably. Slow sex had never done much for me, but this was a transcendent experience and when I came, suddenly and with blinding intensity, I felt like I was drawing him into my body and my soul. He responded to the scream I let out at my climax with a growl and he gave one more hard thrust and released into me. My body milked him and I clung to him, emotion starting to over-whelm me.

He finally opened his eyes and I saw that they were completely orange.

"My mate," he whispered, leaning down to nuzzle my neck and touch a kiss to my shoulder.

"Always," I whispered back, licking the front of his neck.

8

Ty and Samira stayed in bed for the rest of the afternoon, exploring each other as she proved to him again and again that she was everything that he needed, and he showed her over and over that he was everything she could handle. They finally drifted to sleep, completely spent, in each other's arms, but were awaken less than an hour later by frantic pounding on Ty's door.

"This seems awfully familiar," Samira joked as Ty rolled away from her and climbed out of bed, pulling on his pants.

He shot her a smile and walked out into the corridor and then down the stairs. The pounding continued, and Ty was aggravated by the time he reached the door. He didn't want to talk to anybody. He wanted to shuck off his pants and crawl back into bed with Samira.

"What do you want?"

Ero stood on the other side of the door, his expression strained.

"You need to come with me," he said.

"I'm busy right now," Ty said, not really caring what was going on.

Ero shook his head.

"I'm sorry. I know you have Samira here and that's wonderful and I'm sure I'm going to be really happy for you pretty soon, but you need to come with me."

"What's going on?"

Both men turned in the direction of the stairs and Samira's voice. She was walking toward them, buttoning one of Ty's shirts on over her pants. Ty's heart lit up. The shirt engulfed her, but it made her look adorably sexy and completely his. She came to his side and looked at Ero intensely.

"What's going on, Ero?" she repeated.

"The warriors just got back from their patrol. They said that they have really important information and that they need all of us in the meeting hall immediately."

Without hesitation, Ty ran back up the stairs to put on his shoes and shirt. When he got back down, they left the house and hurried toward the meeting hall. Ero was an impossibly fast runner, a skill that had become a tremendous benefit in their last battle against the Klimnu, and he seemed to be struggling to keep himself slow enough that Ty and Samira could keep up with him. Ty knew this meant that something extremely serious was going on with the warriors.

THEY ENTERED the hall and saw it was crowded with Denynso. Several warriors stood on a low stage at one end of the room and Ty saw that Pyra was in the middle, his face stern and concerned. As soon as Ty and Samira settled onto the bench with the other human women, he began to speak.

"We have just returned from our normal patrol, but this time we found something we have never seen before. At the far end of the compound there is a cave in the cliff. Until now we didn't think anything of it. Today, however, we decided to investigate further and found that it is not a cave, but a rock tunnel that dips far into the ground. It was extremely difficult to find and impossible for any of us to navigate because of our size. We believe that this is the way that the Klimnu are getting into the compound. The Traitor told them about the cave and has been providing them with information and resources for quite some time."

A shocked whisper rippled through the crowd and Ty cuddled Samira a little closer to him, part of him terrified that she was going to hear all of this and be afraid and compelled to leave. Instead, she looked fascinated.

"We need to build our defense and devise our plan of attack," Pyra said and sounds of affirmation rose up through the tribe. "It is time we settled this conflict with the Klimnu once and for all."

Ty felt Samira stand up suddenly, causing his arms to drop away from her.

"I'll help," she called out.

There were a few gasps throughout the room and I reached up to pull her back down, but she stayed strong.

"Who is that?" Pyra asked.

"It's me, Samira. I want to help."

TBC

(To be Continued in Part X...)